SARANAC PUBLIC LIBRARY (SAR)
3 1370 00056 8931

D1384673

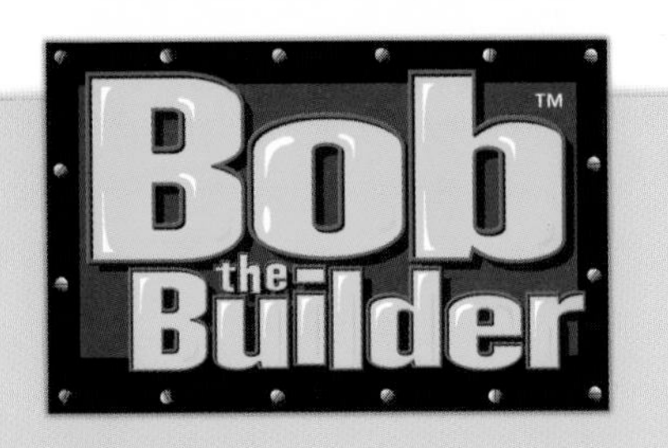

Ready, Set, Race!

adapted by Lauren Forte
based on a script by Diane Redmond

Ready-to-Read

Simon Spotlight

New York London Toronto Sydney

Based upon the television series *Bob the Builder*™
created by HIT Entertainment PLC and Keith Chapman,
as seen on Nick Jr.® Photos by HOT Animation.

SIMON SPOTLIGHT
An imprint of Simon & Schuster Children's Publishing Division
1230 Avenue of the Americas, New York, New York 10020

Manufactured in the United States of America
First Edition
2 4 6 8 10 9 7 5 3 1

Library of Congress Cataloging-in-Publication Data
Forte, Lauren.

Ready, set, race! / adapted by Lauren Forte.— 1st ed.
p. cm. — (Bob the Builder ready-to-read ; #8)
"Based on the TV series Bob the Builder created by HIT Entertainment
PLC and Keith Chapman, as seen on Nick Jr. Photos by HOT Animation."
Summary: Bob, Wendy, and the others have an egg and spoon race.
ISBN 0-689-86497-3 (pbk. : alk. paper)
[1. Racing—Fiction. 2. Trucks—Fiction.] I. Bob the Builder
(Television program) II. Title. III. Series: Bob the builder. Preschool
ready-to-read.
PZ7.A18245 Eg 2004
[E]—dc21
2003006716

"Look, Dizzy," said ,

MRS. PERCIVAL

"  and  are

BOB WENDY

getting ready for the

 and  race."

EGG SPOON

"The winner gets a PIZZA !"

MRS. PERCIVAL added.

“Oh, oh, keep the spoon steady,” said BOB.

“I am trying, Bob,”  WENDY said.

In his yard J.J. was also getting ready for the race.

“Go, Dad!” cheered MOLLY.

Meanwhile  FARMER PICKLES had

a job for  SPUD.

"Please take these  EGGS

to J. J.. He needs them

for cooking."

SPUD took an EGG.

"I want to be in the race too,"

he said.

But his EGG fell to the ground.

"Uh-oh," SPUD said.
"How will I keep my EGG
on my SPOON?"

 SPUD gave the  EGGS to  TRIX.

"These are for  J. J.,"  SPUD said.

"I will race too," said  TRIX.

"See, my fork is like a  SPOON."

But TRIX broke all the EGGS.

"Ooh, what a mess!"

she said.

Later  and 
BOB WENDY
were putting new 
DOORS
on the  shop.
PIZZA
"How is the giant ?"
PIZZA
 asked .
BOB MR. SABATINI

"This [pizza icon] is so big!

PIZZA

It would not have fit

through the old  !"

DOOR

 replied.

MR. SABATINI

 SPUD went to the  PIZZA shop.
He saw  WENDY using putty
to fix the  DOORS.

"I have an idea," said SPUD.

"The putty is sticky. It will keep my EGG on my SPOON."

Soon it was time for

the EGG and SPOON race.

“Ready, set, race!”

 yelled.

MRS. PERCIVAL

started out.
J. J.
"Okay, slow . . . oh no,
I dropped it!"
he cried as his  fell.
EGG

"You cannot catch me!

La, la, la!" yelled SPUD.

 finished first.

SPUD

"I win the !"

PIZZA

"Ohhh, I was close,"

said.

TRIX

“SPUD, your EGG is stuck

to your  SPOON,” said  BOB.

“I used putty,”  SPUD said.

“That is cheating!”

said .

MRS. PERCIVAL

“I am sorry,” said  .

SPUD

" is not the winner,"

SPUD

said .

MRS. PERCIVAL

" is the winner!"

TRIX

"And here is the !"

PIZZA

 said.

MR. SABATINI

“Everybody take a slice!”

said [TRIX]. “Even you, [SPUD].”

"Thanks," said SPUD.

"Mmm, yummy PIZZA!"